ENERGY AND POWER

Lee-Anne Spalding

Bethany, Missouri

Photo Credits:
Cover, Title Page, Pages 5, 6, 7, 9, 21 © constructionphotographs.com; Pages 10, 11 © Rick Rhay; Page 12 ©
Armentrout; Page 13 © Volker Kreinacke; Page 15 © P.I.R.; Page 16 © Glen Jones; Page 17 © Kaupo Kikkas;
Page 19 © Pamela Moore

Cataloging-in-Publication Data

Spalding, Lee-Anne
    Energy and power / Lee-Anne Spalding. — 1st ed.
    p. cm. — (Construction zone science)

    Includes bibliographical references and index.
    Summary: Series offers text and photographs to introduce
science concepts as found at construction sites.
    ISBN-13: 978-1-4242-1378-8 (lib. bdg. : alk. paper)
    ISBN-10: 1-4242-1378-9 (lib. bdg. : alk. paper)
    ISBN-13: 978-1-4242-1468-6 (pbk. : alk. paper)
    ISBN-10: 1-4242-1468-8 (pbk. : alk. paper)

    1. Power resources—Juvenile literature. 2. Energy consumption
—Juvenile literature. 3. Building sites—Juvenile literature.
[1. Power resources. 2. Building sites. 3. Machinery.] I. Spalding, Lee-Anne.
II. Title.
III. Series.
    TJ163.23.S63 2007
    531'.6—dc22

First edition
© 2007 Fitzgerald Books
802 N. 41st Street, P.O. Box 505
Bethany, MO 64424, U.S.A.
Printed in China
Library of Congress Control Number: 2006940872

TABLE OF CONTENTS

TYPES OF ENERGY

You can find many **types** of energy at a **construction site**. Stored energy, heat energy, and energy from movement are just three types of energy. People, **machines**, and tools use energy on the job site.

USING ENERGY

Energy is the power that people, machines, and tools use to do their work. Construction workers use machines and tools that need energy to work.

These workers use energy to move their bodies, too.

GASOLINE ENERGY

Trucks use gasoline to run. Gasoline is a type of stored energy. The gasoline is not used until the truck is turned on.

BATTERY ENERGY

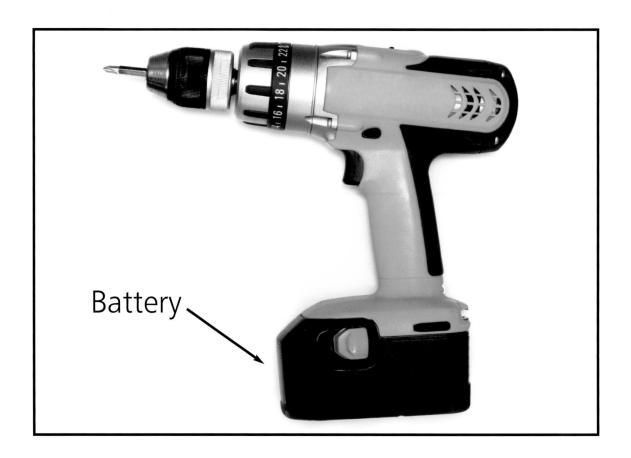

Battery

Batteries are another type of stored energy. Rather than **electricity**, this drill uses a **battery** to run.

Batteries come in many sizes. Large batteries have more energy than small batteries.

MOVING ENERGY

This wrecking ball uses energy from **movement** to work. At a construction site, workers use the wrecking ball to break down old buildings.

This hammer uses moving energy, too. Have you used a hammer? The energy from movement pushes the nail into the wood.

ELECTRICAL ENERGY

Some machines and tools use electricity to work. Generators make electricity. On the job site, generators make the electricity the machines and tools need to do their job.

Generator

HEAT ENERGY

Some construction workers use heat energy. A welder uses heat energy to melt pieces of metal together.

Some welding makes light energy. Can you see the bright light?

ENERGY SAFETY

All kinds of energy are helpful on a construction site. But, it can also be dangerous. Workers must be careful around electrical cords and areas using large amounts of energy!

PEOPLE ENERGY

While using many types of energy, workers also use energy from their bodies. Working, talking, and walking all require energy. People get energy from food.

21.

Construction workers use many types of energy. Stored energy, heat energy, and energy from movement are just three types of energy used at a construction site. This energy helps the workers, machines, and tools do their job!

GLOSSARY

battery (BAT uh ree) — a long-lasting energy source containing alkaline chemicals

construction site (kuhn STRUHKT shun SITE) — a place where workers build

electricity (i lek TRISS uh tee) — electric current

energy (EN ur jee) — power or ability to be active

machine (muh SHEEN) — something that uses energy to help people work

movement (MOOV muhnt) — the act or process of moving

type (TIPE) — a particular kind, class, or group

INDEX

FURTHER READING

Hudson, Cheryl W. *Construction Zone.* Candlewick Press, 2006.
Kilby, Don. *At a Construction Site.* Kids Can Press, 2006.

WEBSITES TO VISIT

Because Internet links change so often, Fitzgerald Books has developed an online list of websites related to the subject of this book. This site is updated regularly. Please use this link to access the list: www.fitzgeraldbookslinks.com/czs/ep

ABOUT THE AUTHOR

Lee-Anne Trimble Spalding is a former public school educator and is currently instructing preservice teachers at the University of Central Florida. She lives in Oviedo, Florida with her husband, Brett, and two sons, Graham and Gavin.